The Berenstain Bears
LEARN ABOUT
STRANGERS

CAUTION

Bear Country is safe.
When every small cub there
Learns some special lessons
From ma and papa bear.

A FIRST TIME BOOK®

The Berenstain Bears LEARN ABOUT STRA...

Stan & Jan Berenstain

Random House 🏠 New York

Copyright © 1985 by Berenstains, Inc. All rights reserved under International and
Pan-American Copyright Conventions. Published in the United States by Random House, Inc.,
New York, and simultaneously in Canada by Random House of Canada Limited, Toronto.

Library of Congress Cataloging in Publication Data: Berenstain, Stan. The Berenstain Bears learn
about strangers. SUMMARY: The Berenstain Bear cubs learn not to be overly friendly with strangers
and give their rules for dealing with them.   1. Children's stories, American.   [1. Strangers—
Fiction.   2. Bears—Fiction.   3. Safety—Fiction]   I. Berenstain, Jan.   II. Title.   PZ7.B4483Bers
1985   [E]   84-43157   ISBN: 0-394-87334-3 (trade); 0-394-97334-8 (lib. bdg.)

Manufactured in the United States of America   1 2 3 4 5 6 7 8 9 0

Brother and Sister Bear, who lived with their mama and papa in the big tree house down a sunny dirt road deep in Bear Country, looked quite a lot alike.

Except for the fact that Brother was a boy cub and Sister was a girl cub, they *were* alike in many ways. And even though they each had hobbies (Brother loved to build and fly model airplanes; Sister had all sorts of special interests), they enjoyed many of the same things: bike riding, baseball, soccer, Frisbee, and just getting out and enjoying nature.

Yes, Brother and Sister were alike in many ways.
But in some important ways they were different.

Brother Bear was cautious and careful
and a little wary of strangers. Sister,
on the other hand, wasn't the least bit
wary. She was friendly to a fault.
Just about everybody
that came her way got a
big hello.

"Hello, butterfly!"

Brother worried about Sister's free and easy way with strangers. Strangers weren't a problem for him. Not talking to strangers suited cautious and careful Brother just fine. But friendly-to-a-fault Sister was different. She talked to *everybody*.

"Sister," said Brother. "You're going to have to stop that!"

"Stop what?" she asked.

"Talking to strangers! It's just not a good idea!"

"Why?" she wanted to know. "Why shouldn't I talk to strangers? What harm is there in it? Is there something *wrong* with strangers?"

"Hmm," said Brother, thinking about it for a moment. "Those aren't questions for a brother. Those are for a mama or papa..."

"Sister Bear, I'm glad you asked those questions!" said Papa Bear, in his deepest and most serious voice. "The reason you should never talk to a stranger and never *ever* take presents from a stranger and never *ever* *ever* go anywhere with a stranger is that it's dangerous."

"What's dangerous about it?" she asked, wide-eyed. "What can happen?"

"Oh, dear," thought Mama Bear. "I *do* hope Papa can tell Sister about strangers without making everything scary."

"All sorts of things!" Papa said. "Here! Look at the newspaper!"

As she looked at it her eyes got wider and wider.

This is what she saw...

"I hope you're paying attention to all this," called Papa to Brother Bear.

"Yes, Papa," said Brother, looking up from his airplanes.

When Sister asked for a bedtime story
that evening, Papa said, "Of course! I
have just the one!"

It was in an old book that Papa had kept since
he was a cub. The story was called "Silly
Goose and Wily Fox." It told how Silly
Goose got into a conversation with Wily Fox, and
before Silly knew quite what was happening
she found herself in Wily's lair. This is
how the story ended:

"'...then there was a snip and a snap and all that was left of Silly Goose was a few floating feathers and a smile on the face of Wily Fox.'"

Sister had a hard time falling asleep that night. Her mind was filled with those headlines. There was even one that said SILLY GOOSE MISSING! WILY FOX QUESTIONED!

STRANGER BOTHERS CUB

MISSING CUB FOUND

CHIEF GRIZZLY

SILLY GOOSE

QUESTIONS

MISSING

STRANGER

WILY FOX

QUESTIONED

The sound of Brother Bear's peaceful breathing finally lulled her to sleep.

The next day dawned bright and friendly—to everybody but Sister. She had spent a restless night and when she looked out the window, everything seemed a little strange. The trees seemed to reach for her, an owl stared at her, and the crows glared.

"Let's go out and ride our bikes on the village green!" said Brother after breakfast. But Sister didn't want to. Brother was puzzled. The green was a bright, busy, friendly place where she loved to play.

"Well, how about some soccer?" But she didn't want to do that either.

It wasn't until he suggested Frisbee, her favorite game, that she agreed to go along.

HOME SWEET TREE

Before they left, they told Mama where they'd be—it was a family rule that they never went anywhere without telling Mama or Papa.

"That's fine," said Mama. "I'm on my way to Farmer Ben's for apples. I'll stop by for you on the way home."

The village green was the same bustling place it had always been. This is what it looked like—*to everyone but Sister.*

This is what it looked like to her. Today even the frogs and butterflies seemed mean and scary to Sister.

Later, when somebody tapped her on the shoulder, she jumped a mile—even though it was just Mama.

YIPE!

"How was everything at the village green?" asked Mama on the way home in the car. Sister sat in front with Mama, and Brother rode in back with the barrel of apples.

"All right, I guess," said Sister. "But there were so many *strangers*!"

Later at home, when Mama and Sister were getting ready to make applesauce, Mama said, "You know, what Papa told you was quite right. It's *not* a good idea to talk to strangers or accept presents or rides from them.

"But," she continued, *"that doesn't mean that all strangers are bad.* Why, chances are, there wasn't a single person on that green that would harm a fly, much less a fine little cub like you. The trouble is...well, it's like this barrel of apples. There's an old saying that goes, 'There'll always be a couple of bad apples in every barrel.' That's the way it is with strangers. Cubs have to be careful because of the few 'bad apples.'"

"Look!" said Sister. "I found one! It's all bumpy and has a funny shape!"

"Well, it certainly is strange looking," said Mama. "But that doesn't necessarily mean it's bad. You can't always tell from the outside which are the 'bad apples.'"

She cut it in half. "See?" she said. "It's fine inside."

"Now, here's one that looks fine on the outside...

—but inside, it's all wormy."
"Yugh!" said Sister.
"What's up?" asked Brother.

"A bad apple!" said Sister.
"Double yugh!" said Brother. "Hey! I'm going to the meadow to fly my new pusher plane. Want to come?"
"Sure," Sister said. "I can pick some wildflowers!" She felt much better now—more like her old friendly self.

The pusher plane was a great
success, and the cubs were about to
head home when someone drove onto
the meadow with a big beautiful orange
and green model airplane.

"Wait!" said Brother. "I want to
watch! It's a radio-controlled job!"

Sister went back to picking wildflowers, but before she knew it, Brother was *talking to the stranger*! For that's what he was, a stranger—no matter how big and beautiful his radio-controlled job was!

She dropped her wildflowers and ran over to them.

"I'm going to send it up and follow in the car," the stranger was saying. "Want to come along?"

"Wow!" said Brother. And he *would* have—if Sister hadn't grabbed his arm and said, "Don't you dare!"

The stranger drove off following his airplane, and Sister ran home shouting, "Brother talked to a stranger! Brother talked to a stranger!"

"But it was a big orange and green radio-controlled job!" said Brother.

"That doesn't matter," said Papa. "We have rules about strangers—and they're important!"

"We have rules about tattletales, too," said Brother, glaring at Sister.

"Sister wasn't tattling. Tattling is telling just to be mean," explained Mama. "And Sister was telling because she loves you and was worried."

"Do you think that fellow was a 'bad apple'?" asked Brother.

"Probably not," said Mama.

"That's right," said Sister. "Most folks are friendly and nice and wouldn't hurt a fly. But *you have to be careful, just in case.*"

"Speaking of apples," said Mama, "how about some of this applesauce I just made?"

As they sat having a dish of Mama's delicious applesauce, Brother and Sister thought about what they had learned that day. There was quite a lot to think about.

For Brother and Sister's Rules for Cubs, turn the page.

BROTHER AND SISTER BEAR'S RULES FOR CUBS

1. *Never talk to a stranger.*

2. *Never take candy or other gifts from a stranger.*

3. *Never ever go anywhere with a stranger.*

4. *Don't keep secrets from your parents— especially if someone asks you to.*

5. *Your body is your own personal property and nobody else's business—especially the private parts. (When you're real little, of course, Mama or Papa may help you with your bath or in the bathroom—and your doctor is in the body business and will have to examine you from time to time, even when you're not little.)*

6. *Use your common sense. We can't have rules for everything. Common sense is what keeps us safe by telling us what to do in situations that are not covered by rules.*